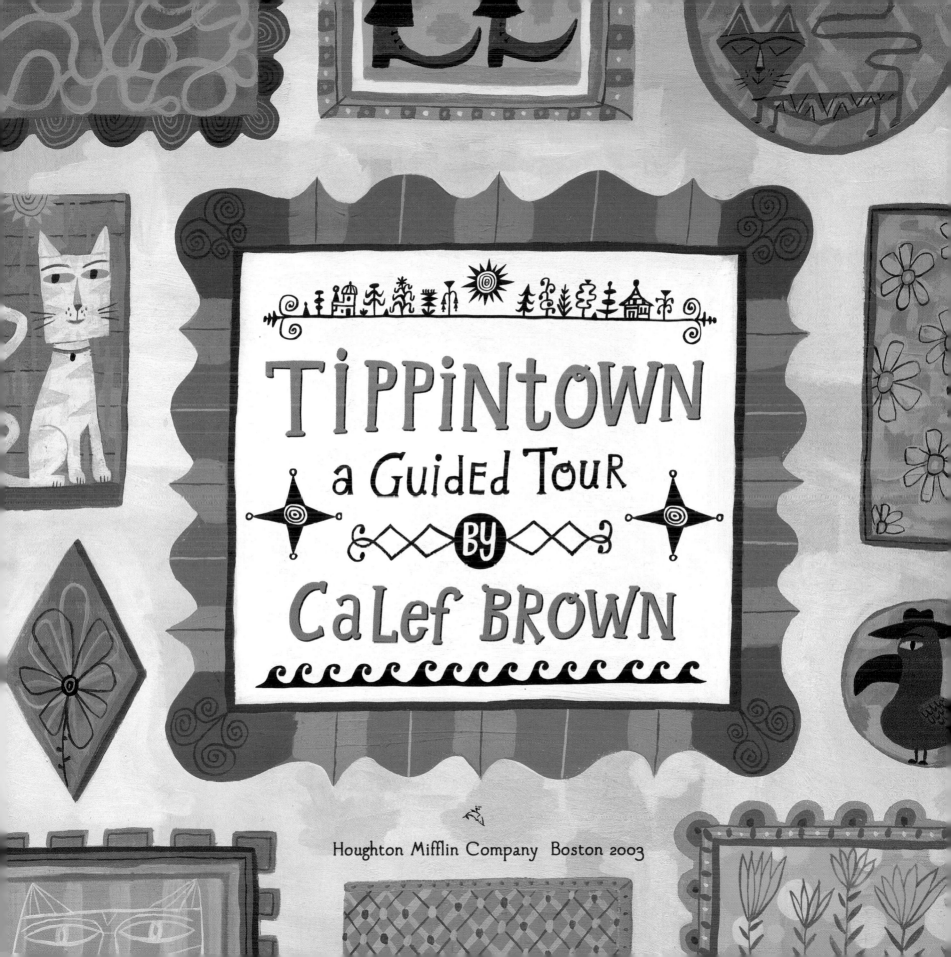

TiPPiNtoWN
a GuidEd ToUR
BY
CaLef BROWN

Houghton Mifflin Company   Boston 2003

for Jenny

Library of Congress Cataloging-in-Publication Data
Brown, Calef.
Tippintown: a guided tour/by Calef Brown
p. cm.
Summary: Invites the reader on a guided tour of a magical land where
mountains speak, dolphins go to school, and a mockingbird plays the lyre.
ISBN 0-618-14972-4
[1. Imaginary places–Fiction. 2. Stories in rhyme.] I. Title.
PZ8.3.B8135 Ti 2003
[E]–dc21
2002000474
WOZ 10 9 8 7 6 5 4 3 2 1

TEN O'CLOCK in Tippintown—
time to take the tour!
Buy yourself a nickel ticket,
stamp it at the door.
Food is all included too,
not a penny more.

I'll be here to fill you in
on all the local lore.

We begin at the famous Amelia statue,
here in Tippin Square.
As most of you know,
Miss Amelia Tippin
invented the folding chair.
Then she became an astronaut,
now she's a millionaire.

I think that's her over there.

Nearby is the Tippin Museum of Art.
The gardens are rather unique.
An excellent place for a tricycle race,
or a game of hide-and-shriek.
The building is open
from seven to seven,
on odd-numbered days of the week.

Let's go take a peek.

Paintings are stacked
from front to back
on every single wall.
Ponder the pictures
of flowers and cats.
Wander down the hall.
Once you've begun
you can't look at just one.
You have to enjoy them all.

It helps if you're really tall.

How would you like
to take a hike?
Let's be on our way.
Tippinoggin Mountain
is about to make your day.
Enormous heads
in purples and reds
are slowly turning gray.

Listen very carefully—
they might have something to say.

Down by the shore
we continue the tour
with a trip in a triple canoe.
Whenever the weather
is warm enough,
it's quite the thing to do.
For an hour or three
on the slippery sea,
we paddle along with the tide.
If the sun gets too hot
in any one spot,
feel free to hop over the side.

Relax and enjoy the ride.

If you go for a swim,
be sure to pop in
on the porpoise graduation.
Every Tippin dolphin
gets a proper education.
They skip the silly speeches
and begin the celebration.

Then they go off to Miami for summer vacation.

Alone on Tippin Island
is a rare Assortment Tree.
The blossoms smell like candy corn
and rutabaga tea.
Leaves and shoots
and flowers and fruits
are various sizes and shapes.
See the luscious artichokes
and multiflavored grapes.

Those are very good
for making crepes.

Speaking of snacks,
it's time for lunch.
What would you like to try?
Macaroni yogurt
on a carrot tulip pie?
How about some sauerkraut
with melted cottage cheese?
Or chewy chocolate enchiladas
stuffed with frozen peas.
Tippinites eat lots and lots
of banana asparagus stew.
Served with sweetened sour sauce,
I think you'll like it too.

It's certainly easy to chew!

Eat up your fill
and c'mon down the hill
for a nice relaxing stroll
Across the Tippin aqueduct
above the napping troll.
On toward the rowdy crowds
and sounds of rock-and-roll.

Just a half a mile or so beyond the distant knoll.

Everyone gathers on Avenue T,
the latest and greatest in style.
The normal routine
is to see and be seen.
We call it "The Wonderful Mile."
Try not to stare at the colorful hair
if you amble around awhile.

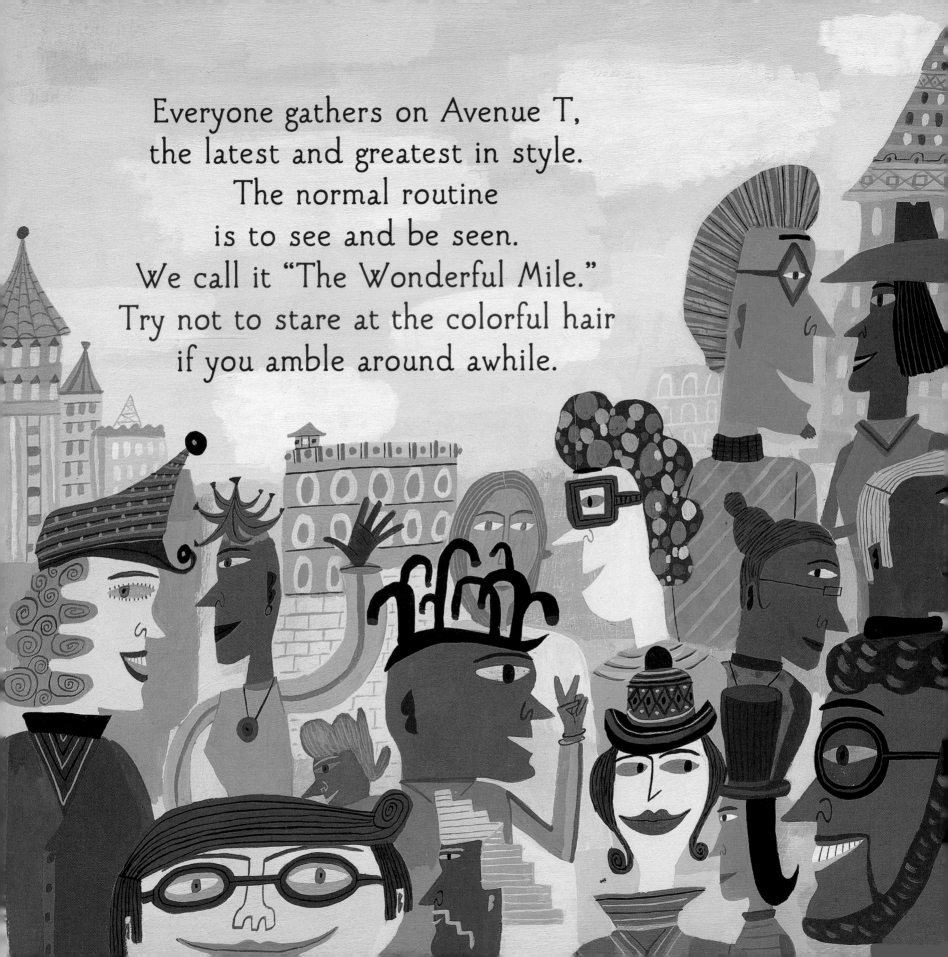

Remember to wear a smile!

All sorts of creatures are out and about,
enjoying a day on the town.
Nothing to fear from the gargoyles here.
They're glad to be safe on the ground.
Up on the edge
of a dangerous ledge
is no place for hanging around.

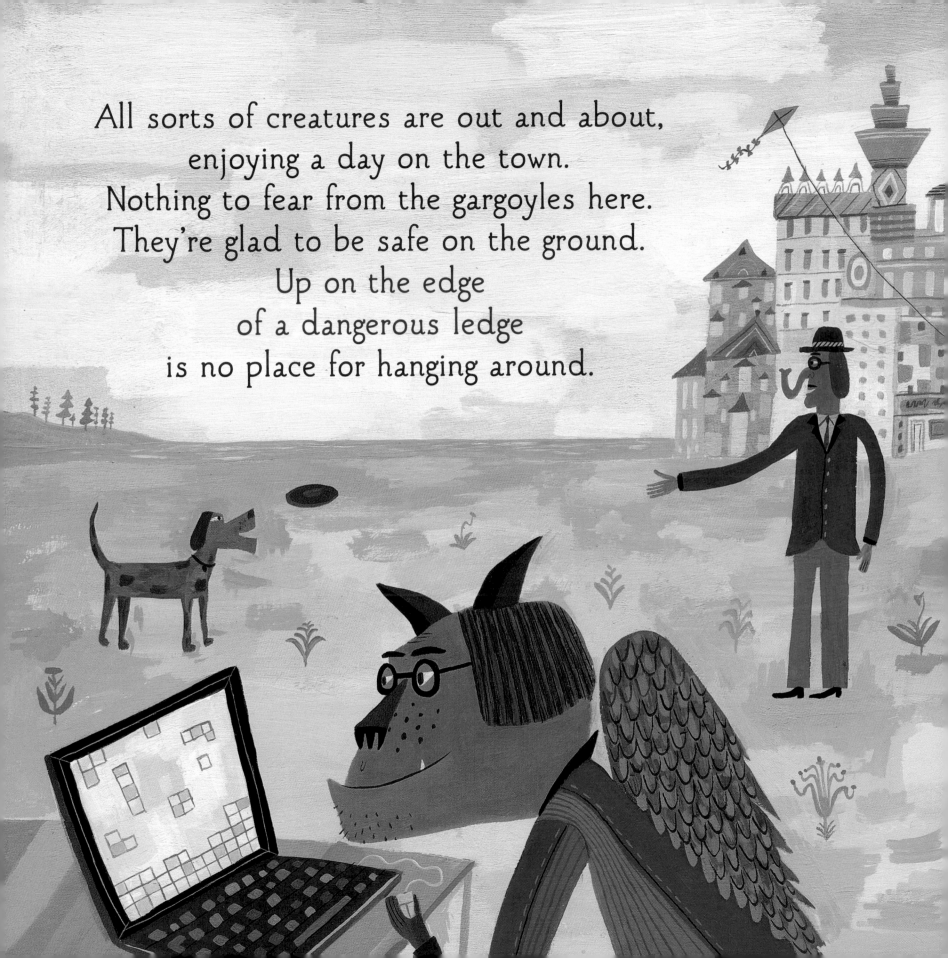

Unless you like tumbling down.

Pull up a seat
for a musical treat.
The Tippinfeather Choir!
Perhaps you've heard
the mockingbird.
He often plays the lyre.
Albatrosses softly sing.
The cranes are known to croon.
The hummingbirds
know all the words
to each and every tune.

I can't say the same for the loon.

We finish the tour
at the Tippintown store
with time for a shopping spree.
Shirts and caps and coffee cups
as far as the eye can see.
All the souvenirs in here
come with a guarantee.

Tippintown is winding down—
the sun has nearly set.
I'm glad that you could make it.
So delighted that we met.
You and I must say goodbye,
but don't be too upset . . .

Tomorrow's tour is sure to be your greatest journey yet!